DOVER 3D Coloring CRAZY CHRISTMAS

Jessica Mazurkiewicz

3-D GLASSES INSIDE!

DOVER PUBLICATIONS, INC.
MINEOLA, NEW YORK

Note

Brighten your Christmas season with this 3-D Coloring Book featuring full-page patterns created from traditional yuletide imagery. Highlights include gingerbread men, reindeer, nutcracker dolls, ornaments, candles, Santa Claus, and more! Each pattern is enclosed inside a detailed border for a finished look. The 30 black-and-white 3-D images created by artist Jessica Mazurkiewicz will make a distinctive holiday project for colorists of all ages.

Copyright

Copyright © 2011 by Dover Publications, Inc.
All rights reserved.

Bibliographical Note

3-D Coloring Book—Crazy Christmas is a new work, first published by
Dover Publications, Inc., in 2011.

International Standard Book Number
ISBN-13: 978-0-486-48409-9
ISBN-10: 0-486-48409-2

Manufactured in the United States by Courier Corporation
48409202
www.doverpublications.com

1

3

11

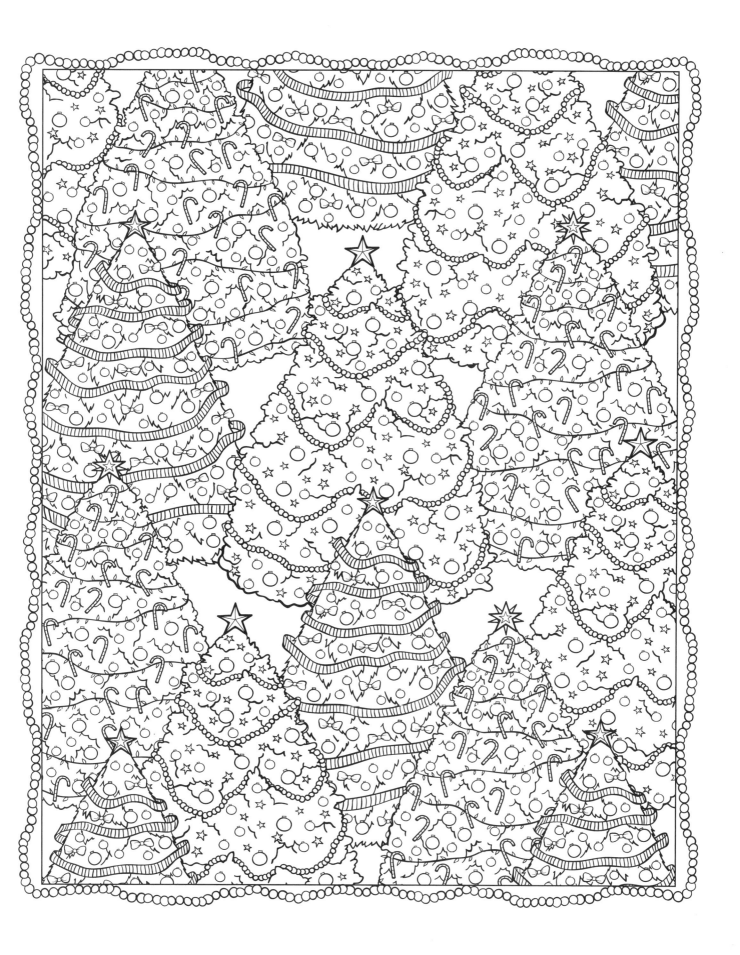

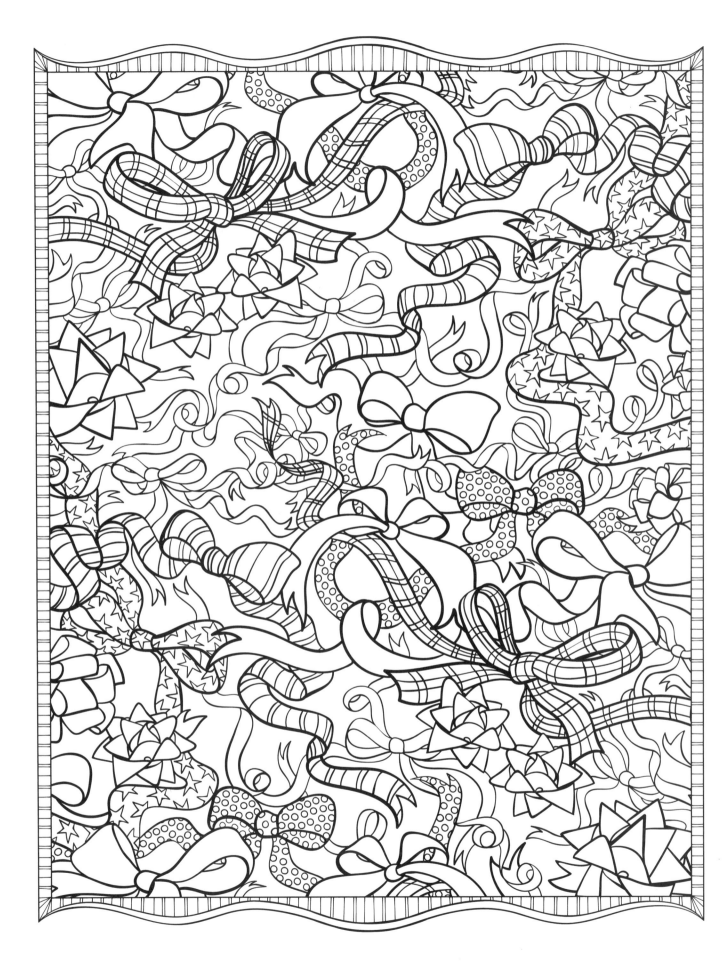

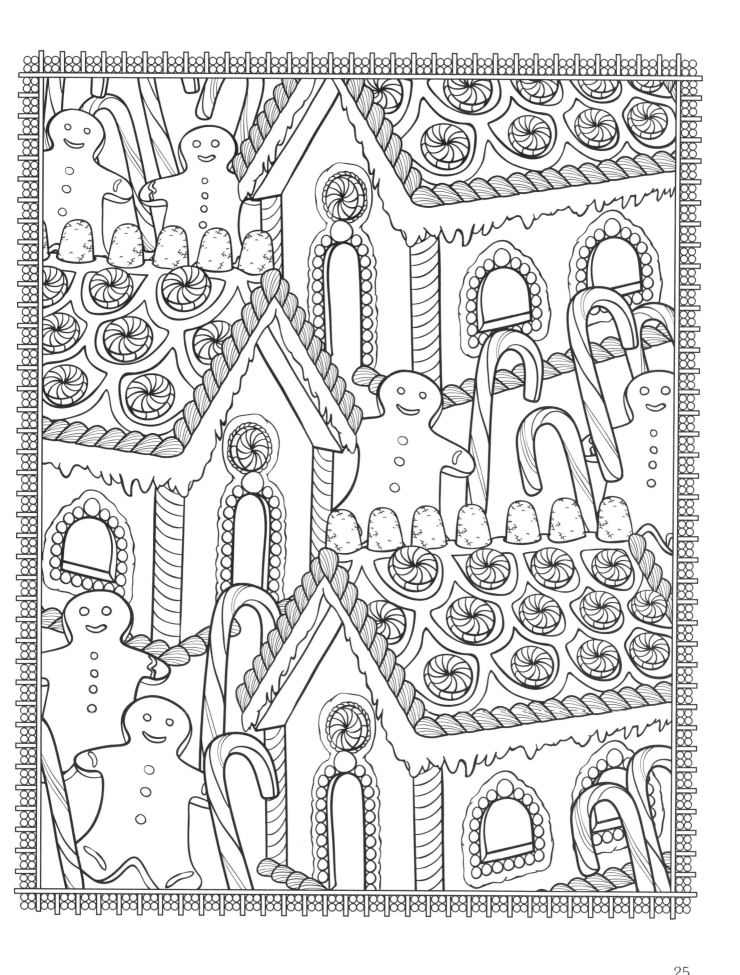

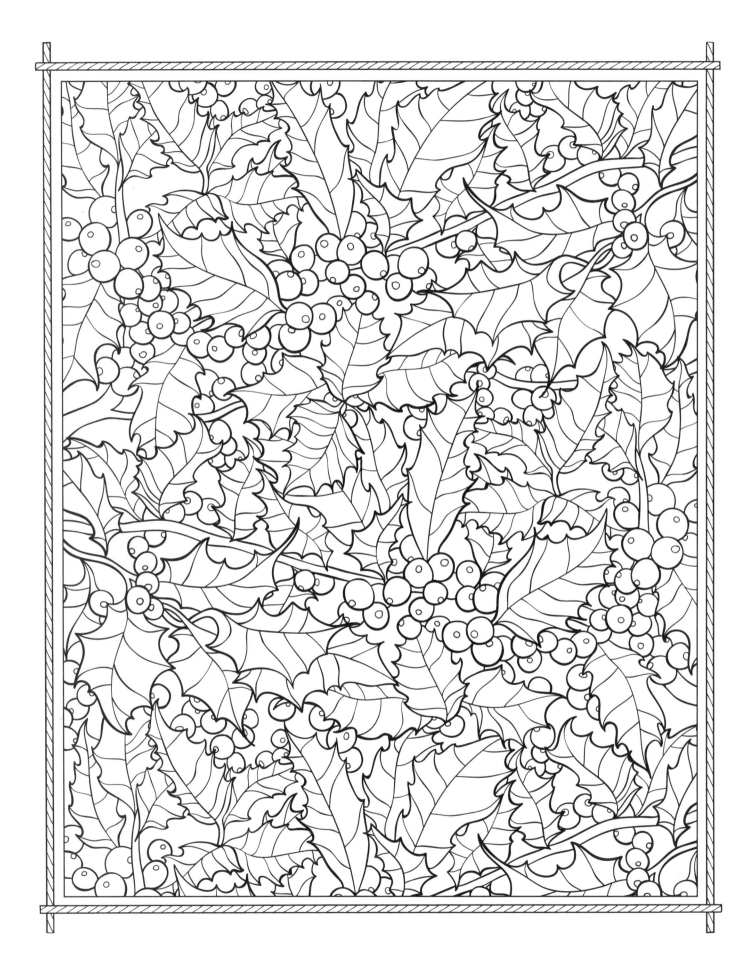